Pig on a Plane

Story
Irene Magers

Illustrations
Amelia Farrin

PLAY HOUSE BOOKS
An imprint of Shady Tree Press

For Theo

Story copyright © 2024 by Irene Magers
Illustrations copyright ©t 2024 by Amelia Farrin

Cover and Book Design by Scribe Freelance

Published by Play House Books, a division of Shady Tree Press
shadytreepress@gmail.com

All rights reserved, including the right to reproduce this book or portions thereof in any form whatsoever. No part of this book may be reproduced or used in any manner without the prior written permission of the copyright owners, except for the use of brief quotations in a book review.

ISBN: 978-0-9841211-9-9

First Edition, 2024

Printed in the United States

Each spring, Maisie the pig had five piglets. Sometimes she even surprised the Jensen family with six or seven.

Maisie was wonderful.

But this spring she only had one piglet. One single piglet and he was small.

It was a big disappointment for everyone on the farm, especially for the Jensen children who always looked forward to caring for the piglets.

The Jensen family gathered by Maisie's stall to welcome the little piglet, all the while wondering what had gone wrong. One single piglet would not help the farm prosper.

Especially since there had been little precipitation during the winter and no April showers, which meant some crops might fail.

Disregarding his scrawny appearance, the children loved the new piglet nonetheless.

They named him Bruno, figuring that such a strong name might lend stature to his small pink body.

With only one piglet to care for, the Jensen children had more time to spend with him, often taking him into the house.

How they laughed the day he stood up on his hind legs and walked around the kitchen table just like the rest of them.

In fact, Bruno soon began to think of himself as one of the children and followed them everywhere, mimicking their gestures and expressions.

Every afternoon, standing on his two hind legs, he waited patiently for the school bus to drop them off at the farmhouse gate.

When neighboring children came to play, Bruno was always included.

He learned to catch a ball and, running on his hind legs, could break into a sprint like the best of them.

Invariably there was an argument about who got to have Bruno on their team.

Halloween came. The Jensen children dressed Bruno in blue jeans, boots, a plaid shirt, and tucked his ears into a cowboy hat.

He carried his own treat bag and in the dim evening light people thought he was just another child and dropped candy into his bag.

When he grunted something that sounded like "thank you" they smiled, believing him to be a very polite child.

When Maisie became ill that winter, the veterinarian came to take her to the animal hospital and Bruno was moved into the house to live with the children, which suited everyone fine.

The farm was a happy place.

However, the drought in the Jensen's Idaho valley continued.

Eventually, they had no choice but to sell their farm and move to Utah where Mr. Jensen got a job working on someone else's farm.

A sad situation that became even sadder when the children learned they would not be taking Bruno with them.

The buyer of the Jensen's farm insisted the pig stay behind along with the two cows, one horse, five chickens and a rooster.

The day the Jensens moved away it rained tears. The children cried and Bruno made choking sounds when they hugged him good-by.

The children's wet faces were plastered against the car's back window as they waved to Bruno until the distance grew so great they could no longer see him standing at the farm house gate.

Once the car was out of sight, Bruno walked, head down, into the farm house and, as was his habit, got into his bed.

This did not suit the new owners who did not think that a pig should live in the house, let alone sleep in a bed.

They took him out to the barn to be with the two cows, the horse, the chickens and the rooster.

Bruno missed the children. Weeks went by. He lost weight.

The new owner spoke with his wife about "bringing him to market" before he became too thin to fetch a good price.

They were not impressed with his ability to walk on his hind legs and make sounds that seemed to say "thank you" and "hi."

Bruno, in his wisdom, realized his days on the farm were numbered. He made a decision. He must run away and try to find the Jensens.

Before their departure, he had heard them talk about a place called Utah. The word stuck in his head.

One day while the new owners were in town, Bruno entered the house and found a box of old clothes that the Jensens had left behind.

The blue jeans and shirt he'd worn for Halloween were in the box. So were the boots. The cowboy hat was gone but, rummaging around, he found a baseball cap. He took everything out to the barn.

Early the next morning before anyone on the farm was awake, Bruno got dressed, tucked his ears into the baseball cap, and left.

Walking down the road on his hind legs, the driver of a vegetable truck stopped and, mistaking him for a boy, offered him a ride.

Grunting his best simulation of "thank you," Bruno remained in the truck all the way to the Idaho Falls Airport where the driver was making a delivery.

Wondering what to do next, Bruno jumped from the truck, now strolling around the busy airport on his two hind legs.

Suddenly a loudspeaker announced a flight to Salt lake City, Utah.

Utah was a word Bruno recognized. He perked up and as people bunched together, filing through security into the terminal and toward the designated gate, he mingled with a family traveling with several children.

His comfort zone.

The mother was holding a crying baby while her two boys shoved each other and argued loudly.

The father told them in no uncertain terms to behave and now handed a distracted gate attendant a fistful of boarding passes, which were scanned but not carefully counted.

That's how Bruno got on the flight.

He took a seat next to one of the boys sitting with the father. The other boy was sitting across the aisle with the mother and the baby.

When a late-boarding passenger stopped at Row 17 and checked his seat assignment, he turned to a flight attendant, telling her that a boy occupied his seat.

She was about to ask Bruno for his boarding pass when the man decided he'd rather not sit among children and asked if she could find him a seat elsewhere. She did.

The plane took off. Snacks were served.

Bruno had apple juice, slurping so loudly the boy next to him made faces at his bad manners.

The baby had stopped crying, was now asleep, and the parents finally seemed to notice the strange boy sitting in their row. Apparently, he was traveling alone.

Whispering to each other, they agreed he looked rather odd, certainly not a very handsome child. His nose was too big, his arms were too short and while they couldn't see his feet for the boots, they thought his hands looked deformed.

They clucked to each other in sympathy with his "handicap."

The flight droned on. Bruno had been up early and, tired, dozed off. As he slept his baseball cap slipped off, exposing his ears.

The boy sitting next to him looked more closely at Bruno and pulled at his father's sleeve.

"Daddy!" he said. "There's a pig next to me." Inattentive, the father shrugged and continued working on his laptop. The boy raised his voice.

"There's a pig on the plane!" he now said so loudly that a flight attendant heard and figured a passenger had spilled something. She came down the aisle.

"Oh!" she exclaimed, reaching Row 17. "My goodness! It is a pig!"

Another flight attendant approached. His eyes popped. He immediately turned and hurried to report to the Captain. Unconvinced, the Captain sent his First Officer to investigate what was probably just a prank.

However, arriving at Row 17, one look told the First Officer that this sleeping passenger was, indeed, a pig. He rushed back to the flight deck.

The Captain went on the intercom to inquire if anyone was flying with a service animal in the form of a pig. There was no response except some giggling among the passengers.

What kind of a nut would travel with a pig?

The Captain tried again. "Has anyone's pet escaped from it's carrier?"

No one claimed the pig. But of course now everyone wanted to see the pig and began milling around Row 17.

An attendant alerted the flight deck to the growing crowd in the aisle. The Captain turned on the "fasten your seatbelt" sign and told everyone to please return to their seats.

The goings-on had woken Bruno. Rubbing his eyes, he calmly replaced the baseball cap on his head.

Discussion on the flight deck between the Captain and his First Officer centered around the question: How had a pig gotten onto the plane?

The Captain checked the manifest. No pig or any other domestic animal was listed in the cargo hold. Besides, how could it have escaped its crate and made it into the main cabin?

Impossible.

Finally the Captain left the flight deck and walked back to Row 17 to see for himself, all the while thinking that the pig was surely just a figment of someone's imagination.

Feeling refreshed after his nap, Bruno looked up at the Captain looking down at him. He held up his hand for a high-five like the children on the farm had taught him.

Astonished, the Captain blinked and mumbled, "Hi there, Buddy."

"Hi!" Bruno replied, adding a distinct "thank you." While those two words always seemed to please people, this Captain turned quite pale.

"Did you hear the pig speak?" he asked the two flight attendants standing by. When both nodded in the affirmative, the Captain rushed back to the flight deck to radio Ground Control.

"West Air Flight 1704," he said when Ground Control picked up the radio sequence. "We have a pig onboard."

"There's usually one on every flight," the controller chuckled.

"No. I mean . . . Really! We have a pig on the plane. Dressed like a boy. Pants, shirt, boots. Baseball cap. And he . . . he speaks!"

The controller rolled his eyes. He consulted other controllers. They checked their computer screens. No pig—speaking or otherwise—was listed on any flight or in any cargo hold.

The controllers began to wonder if perhaps the Captain had worked too many hours and was suffering from fatigue or . . . worse. They requested a word with the First Officer.

The First Officer got on the line and corroborated everything the Captain had said, except the part about the pig speaking, which he had not heard.

With a level-headed First Officer, Ground Control decided the flight was in no danger and could continue to its destination.

The controller tracking the flight signed off and immediately called Animal Rescue in Salt Lake City.

"Hey listen," he said, getting a woman from Animal Rescue on the line. "There's a pig on West Air Flight 1704. Can you meet the plane at the gate and remove the animal?"

"Sure," the woman said and couldn't help but ask, "How did a pig get on the plane?"

"No one seems to know," the controller said.

"How large is the pig?" the woman wanted to know.

"The Captain didn't say. But he told me it's wearing clothes and it talks."

The woman laughed. "Maybe we'd better send someone to remove the Captain. He sounds bonkers!"

After hanging up, the woman decided to call her brother. He worked for a local newspaper.

"Hey, Luke!" she said. "I got a hot tip for you."

"Great!" Luke said. It had been a slow day. "Gimme the scoop!"

And that's how Luke, the reporter, along with his film crew came to be in the Salt Lake City airport terminal, waiting for West Air Flight 1704 to arrive.

Once the plane landed, the Captain requested passengers to please remain seated while the pig was being removed.

That last word was redundant because Bruno did not need to be removed.

Nice as can be, he got out of his seat and walked off the plane with a polite "thank you" to the Captain and First Officer standing by the cockpit door.

Burly Animal Rescue personnel were rushing the jet bridge with nets and prods.

These were unnecessary precautions because—walking calmly on his hind legs—the pig seemed to pose no threat to anyone.

The men stopped and gaped at the sight of him. Bruno held up his hand for a hi-five. Now that he was in Utah, perhaps these nice people might help him find the Jensens.

With the Animal Rescue team trailing him, Bruno entered the terminal where word of a pig on a plane had spread and drawn curious onlookers. The minute Luke spotted Bruno, he and his film crew jumped into action.

Elbowing through the people and getting next to this amazing pig, Luke spoke into a microphone while his crew recorded the event. Cameras rolled and lights flashed.

Once the pig was led away, Luke interviewed a flight attendant and several passengers.

That afternoon the story of a pig on a plane was on the front page of every newspaper across Utah.

That same afternoon when Mrs. Jensen went to check the mailbox by the road and to meet the school bus, she picked up the newspaper lying in the driveway.

The bus came, the children got off and walked subdued into the house; subdued because although weeks had passed, coming home from school wasn't the same without Bruno waiting for them.

After washing their hands, the children sat down at the kitchen table to eat muffins and apple slices.

Mrs. Jensen left the mail and the paper on the table for Mr. Jensen to look at when he came home from work.

Bobby the oldest, glanced at the newspaper. Suddenly he grabbed it, almost tearing it in two.

"Bobby!" his mother admonished. "Don't ruin the paper before your father has read it."

Bobby didn't hear her. He was hollering and pointing. "Look! Look!" he cried, jumping up and down. "Bruno! It's Bruno!"

Now everyone wanted to see the paper. Sure enough, there was Bruno on the front page.

The bold headline over the photo said:

PIG ON A PLANE

Underneath was an article that Bobby excitedly read aloud. The article ended by asking anyone who recognized the pig to please come forward.

Mrs. Jensen ran from the house to find her husband. Minutes later both returned to the kitchen, breathless.

After seeing the paper, Mr. Jensen made a phone call and, minutes later, everyone piled into the family car and drove at the speed of light to the Animal Rescue Center in Salt Lake City.

They found Bruno in an attractive, clean pen.

Happiness ruled the day for Bruno and the Jensens. For Luke and his film crew as well because they were on hand at the rescue center to record the joyful reunion for another front page article.

The Jensens took Bruno home and into their house, not the barn. The owner of the farm could hardly object. After all, who could deny such a remarkable pig a comfortable bed.

But that was not all.

A publisher from New York soon paid the Jensens a visit. When the book about Bruno's adventures came out, a movie producer from Hollywood paid a visit as well.

The result was that the Jensens could now buy back their old, beloved Idaho farm with enough money left over to install irrigation to mitigate future droughts.

Best of all, Bruno could reclaim his spot at the gate where he once again waited every afternoon for the children to come home from school.

www.ingramcontent.com/pod-product-compliance
Lightning Source LLC
LaVergne TN
LVHW072334040525
810280LV00009B/47